Jane Clarke

illustrated by Britta Teckentrup

TIPTOE TIGER

nosy crow

An imprint of Candlewick Press

The sun is going down in the jungle,
but Tara is wide awake.

All she wants to do is bounce and pounce!

There's time for one more game
before bedtime. But who will want to play?

Look!
Can you see someone over there
with beautiful, bright wings?

It's a butterfly and her friends!

But will they want to
bounce and pounce?

Let's tell Tara to tiptoe up quietly
so she doesn't scare them away.

Whisper, **"Tiptoe, tiger."**

Oh, no. Tara didn't tiptoe.
Her big pounce frightened
all the butterflies.

Can you flutter your arms
up and down really fast?

You can!

But look!
Who's that over there with
the colorful feathers?

It's a peacock!

Look at all his pretty colors.
Which one is your favorite?

Now, we'd better tell Tara
not to scare the peacock.

Whisper, **"Tiptoe, tiger."**

Uh-oh!

Tara bounced and pounced . . .

and frightened the peacock away.

But look! There's a tail
dangling down from a tree.

Can you stretch your arms wide
to show how long it is?

Who do you think the tail belongs to?

It's a monkey!

But we forgot to tell Tara to tiptoe!
And now the monkey is swinging off
through the trees.

It's getting dark.
Look—the owl family has come out
to watch the moon.

How many owls can you count?

We'd better tell Tara to tiptoe.

Can you whisper, **"Tiptoe, tiger"**?

Good job. Tara listened that time!

And can you hear the owls hooting?
Hoo, hoo! Hoo, hoo!

Can you hoot too?

Oh, dear. Tara can't hoot,
but she can roar . . .

Rooaaar!

Look!
All the owls are flying away!

I bet you can roar just as loudly as Tara.

After all that roaring,
Tara needs a drink.
But who's that lurking in
the middle of the river?

Look out!
It's a crocodile!

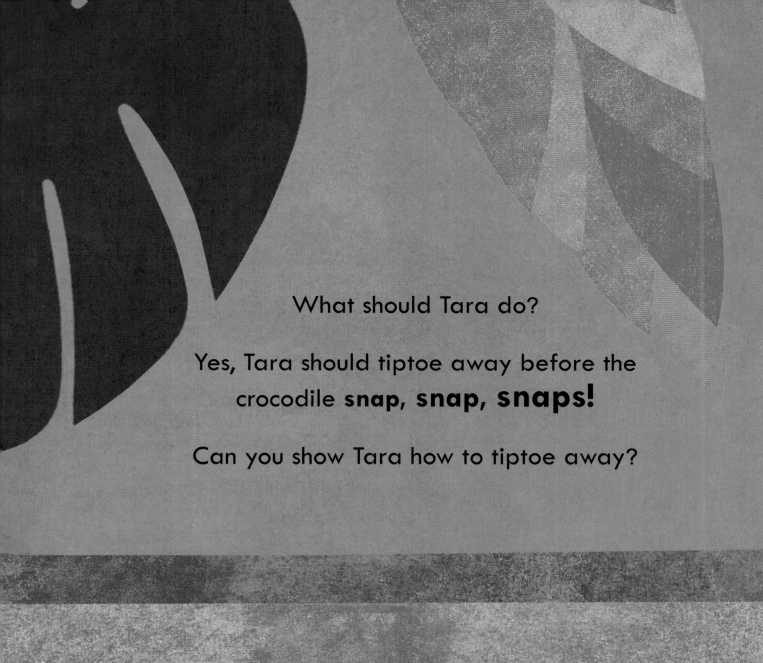

What should Tara do?

Yes, Tara should tiptoe away before the crocodile **snap, snap, snaps!**

Can you show Tara how to tiptoe away?

Come on, let's say, **"Tiptoe, tiger!"**

You did it!

Tara is tiptoeing away
as fast as she can.

But she's not looking where she's going.
Watch out, Tara!

BUMP!

It's Tara's mommy!
Tara is happy to be home.
After all that bouncing and pouncing,
she is feeling sleepy.

All she wants to do now is cuddle up with her mommy.

Can you yawn like a tired tiger cub?

Yaaawwwn.

And now it's time for bed.

Let's tiptoe away and whisper,
"Night, night, little tiger. Sleep tight!"

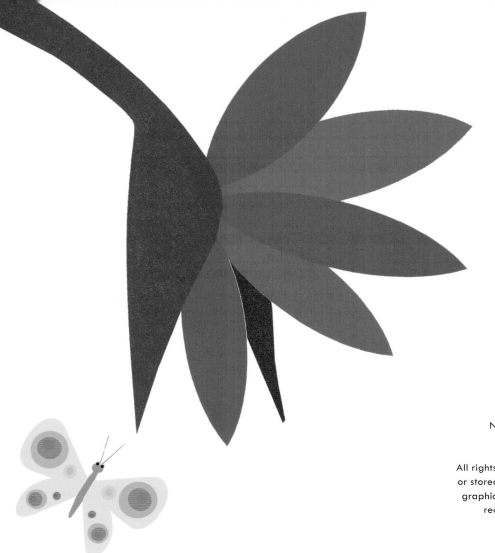

To my four
granddaughters, with love
JC

To Irina
BT

First US edition 2022

First published by Nosy Crow Ltd. (UK) 2021

Library of Congress Catalog Card Number 2022930413
ISBN 978-1-5362-2750-5

22 23 24 25 26 27 APS 10 9 8 7 6 5 4 3 2 1

Printed in Humen, Dongguan, China

This book was typeset in TW Cen MT Pro.
The illustrations were created digitally.

Nosy Crow
an imprint of
Candlewick Press
99 Dover Street
Somerville, Massachusetts 02144
www.nosycrow.com
www.candlewick.com